ESCAPADE JOHNSON
and
MAYHEM AT MOUNT
MOOSILAUKE

written by
Michael Sullivan

illustrated by
Joy Kolitsky

Big Guy Books, Inc.
Carlsbad, California

Published by BiG GUY BOOKS, Inc.
6359 Paseo Del Lago • Ste B
Carlsbad, CA 92011 USA

Printed in USA

ISBN: 1929945701

Library of Congress: 2006920444

Check out all the NEW STUFF at www.bigguybooks.com

INTRODUCTION

Hi. My name is Escapade Johnson. No, that's not a nickname; my parents actually named me Escapade. Something having to do with when they were in college. I don't really get it, but that's the name they gave me. Well, not the whole name. If they had been kind they would have given me a middle name that I could use. But my dad wanted to name me after my uncle Chester, so my name really is Escapade Chester Johnson. I'll stick with Escapade.

The funny thing is the name doesn't even fit. I mean, Escapade? I'm the most boring kid at Sanbornton Elementary School, which is in the most boring town in New Hampshire. Which, come to think of it, might be the most boring state in the country. There are just two paved roads in town. TWO! And only one of them has a line down the middle of it. The most exciting thing that happened here in the last ten years was when a moose ate all the ballots during the last election. Sadly, that was my fault. But that's another story.

You see, I may only be eleven years old, but I know what I want to do with my life. I want to be a writer. But what do you write about when you live in a dull little town like this? Well, you write what you can with what inspiration you have and hope for the best, I guess. So I'll tell you about the field trip the fifth-grade of Sanbornton Elementary School took to climb Mount Moosilauke, complete with bear poop, a poisonous belt, teddy bear underwear, and a peanut butter sandwich that saved the day.

Enjoy.

Chapter 1

"**A** mountain!" cried Cherilyn Travis. "What do I look like, a lumberjack?"

Pink shoes, pink socks too, polka dot sun dress—forty-eight pounds of elementary school model with a pink bow in her hair. Cherilyn looked like anything but a lumberjack. Of course, most lumberjacks are more warm and cuddly than Cherilyn. Still, ho-doggy she could drive me up a tree. Me and about twenty other fifth-grade boys from the number of spitballs that flew in her direction every day. You see, Cherilyn had a way of being in the center. No matter what, it seemed the rest of us fifth-graders were always looking, talking, or even aiming, at Cherilyn.

"Now Cherilyn," cooed Mrs. Bartgauer, who doted on her just as every teacher since first-grade had. "It'll be fun. You'll be out in the fresh air, getting some real exercise –"

"Skipping school!" chimed in Jimmy Whitehorse, who seemed to have only taken a few minutes to register what this proposed field trip really meant. This was pretty quick thinking for Jimmy, who generally didn't bother with thinking, not when there were substitute teachers to lock in the boiler room, hair nets to fill with bugs before the cafeteria ladies could put them on, and second-graders to chase up trees with his enormous dogs.

"We can count bird species and make nature drawings," called out Melinda Trackson. Everyone, even Mrs. Bartgauer, glared at her. This was just the kind of thing you would expect Melinda to say. She had missed the important part of the whole deal and was concentrating on school work when she should have been excited about goof-off time. Nobody likes a suck up.

"Will we get to sleep in tents?" called a boy from the back. It was Benny Black, who probably had never seen a tent. He had moved to

Sanbornton from New York a year ago. Rumor had it that Benny slept in a huge bed with four posts at the corners and a huge cloth draped over the whole thing. Maybe he thought that was what a tent was like. The rest of us knew better.

"I am NOT sleeping in a tent," said Cherilyn, who actually stood up so she could plant her fists on her hips.

Katrina Finink stood up and said, "Me neither," which was her favorite phrase, usually said right after Cherilyn had spoken. Tall and thin, in a skirt that reached to the floor, Katrina shouldn't have had trouble standing out, especially in a little mud town like this. But there was always Cherilyn, front and center, and Katrina was always a step behind.

It was what my dad calls a "love-hate"

relationship. Katrina wanted what Cherilyn had but never seemed to know how to get it, so she hung around trying to be like her. She liked to repeat things after Cherilyn. It kept her from having to make up her own stuff to say. Katrina always looked like she wanted to be in the middle of things, even if it meant being hit by spitballs.

"Yea, an overnight! We'll miss two whole days of school!" Jimmy actually leapt onto the top of his desk, slipped, fell head first onto the tile floor, bounced, landed on his butt, bounced again, and was back on his feet pumping his fist in the air. I think he was warming to the idea.

The class erupted. Kids left their desks and gathered in pockets, voices rising in excited conversation, as if this early September field trip was a matter of national importance. Mrs.

Bartgauer was losing control. Usually it was almost lunch time before she had to scream at the top of her lungs to get anyone to listen to her.

"Children, children! Now settle down. Climbing Mount Moosilauke will be an experience that all of you will treasure. I can't wait to hear all about it when you get back."

The class went quiet. Everyone seemed to know there was something wrong about the teacher's statement, but we weren't quite sure what it was. Marjorie Jackson figured it out first.

"You're not coming with us?" she asked. Marjorie's hands began to shake nervously, and everyone near her inched away. Marjorie's hands were known to break things: bottles, chairs, bones. She didn't mean to. Marjorie tried as hard as she could to be very gentle and graceful. It didn't work. Her hands seemed to have a mind of their own, and that mind was pretty warped.

Mrs. Bartgauer went as pink as Cherilyn's socks. I don't think she had planned on telling us she wasn't going. At the moment, it should have been the most logical conclusion in the world. Mrs. Bartgauer was a woman of imposing stature. I knew that because that's what my dad had said once when he was trying to describe her to a business friend. She was taller than my dad and looked perfectly rectangular in her long, flowered cotton dress, one of about a dozen she seemed to own that differed only in the color of the flowers. I couldn't imagine her climbing a mountain.

"Why, no," she said, her voice getting crackly the way it did sometimes when Jimmy said something about his family. "I'm afraid I'm a bit...er...advanced in years to go parading up a mountain."

"You're sending us up there alone?" Katrina cried, tears filling her eyes. "We'll get lost. We'll be eaten by bears. We'll have to build houses in trees and eat bugs!"

"Now Katrina, don't get hysterical. Of course I won't send you up there alone. Mr. Hauteman, Ms. Jensen, and," she hesitated, "Mr. Dobson will be taking you."

Mr. Dobson, the balding, paunch-gutted gym teacher. He called everyone's moms "Babe." He ruffled the hair of every boy he had ever had in gym class, even when they were thirty years old. He wore plaid sports coats over his sweats when he arrived at school each day. His breath always smelled like a spicy Italian sandwich and he got way too close when he talked to you.

"I am not going out into the wilderness with that creep," said Cherilyn. Nobody had to ask which teacher she meant.

"I'm not either," said Katrina, the tears frozen at the edges of her eyes.

"Cherilyn, I will not have you speaking about a teacher like that just because..." Mrs. Bartgauer thought better and left the sentence unfinished. "Anyways, it will work like any other field trip. Mr. Hauteman will be in charge, and we will ask for some parents to go, too." She began handing out permission forms. "Now, when your parents sign this, ask them to check the box at the bottom if they would like to chaperone."

She stopped just then in front of Jimmy and gave a little shudder, hesitated, but finally handed him a form. I guess it dawned on her that Jimmy's parents were unlikely to volunteer to climb a mountain with a bunch of fifth-graders, and even if they did, she would not have to witness it.

CHAPTER 2

You may have noticed that I wasn't part of all that. I was sitting quietly at my desk doodling in my notebook a mountain covered with bears, werewolves, poisonous snakes, giant acid-belching lizards, Bigfoot, Mr. Dobson, and other frightening creatures. Fires, freak snowstorms, flash floods, attacks by pigmy cannibals. What were they sending us out into? I know we had been hard on Mrs. Bartgauer, but she had to be expecting it. Every teacher in school knew about this class; three had retired the year before we hit their grades, and one of them was twenty-seven years old.

Sure, Jimmy had taken all the screws out of Mrs. Bartgauer's chair and then balanced it in place, just ready to collapse when she sat on it. And, yes, Benny Black had brought his pet cockroaches to school in a box whose lid wasn't as secure as it should have been. Cherilyn and Katrina had glued Davy Gilman's pants to his chair, and Mrs. Bartgauer had found out something she didn't want to know about what

Davy wore for underwear. Was that enough to justify sending thirty eleven-year-olds to almost certain and grisly death? Apparently, it was.

During gym class, Mr. Dobson handed out instruction lists for what we should bring. No tents, as it turns out the entire hike wouldn't take more than five hours. Jimmy scanned the list quickly and raised a hand.

"Mr. Dobson, shouldn't we bring a machete to cut through the underbrush?"

"This is New Hampshire, Jimmy, not the Amazon jungle, and the path has already been cleared. Besides, where would any of us get a machete?"

Jimmy's hand was back up in a heartbeat. Mr. Dobson suddenly looked frightened and went on to the next question.

"Will we have mules to carry this stuff," asked Benny, "or will we be using native porters?"

"Hey! Around here, I'm a native," said Davy Gilman, "and I'm not carrying your stuff anywhere."

Benny may not have lived in New Hampshire very long, but Davy had lived in this very town for his whole life. So had his father. So had his grandfather. The only Gilman male to leave Sanbornton in the last hundred years was Davy's great grandfather who joined the army three days before the end of World War I. He was back in town in a week. Davy called anyone from more than two towns away a "flatlander", just like his father. And his grandfather.

Mr. Dobson jumped between them. "Everyone carries their own gear. Besides, this is just a day hike. You carry more weight than that in books every day."

"Then maybe someone will carry mine for me," said Cherilyn, and she was looking at me! She winked; she actually winked. My legs went all wobbly. Sure, I said to myself, I'll carry your books, and clean your room, and wash your parents car, and anything else you ask me to do. Of course, after that she'll probably just hold hands with Benny so she can ride in his father's Mercedes. I think I'm going to be sick.

"Everyone carries their own gear," Mr. Dobson repeated. "It won't be that heavy."

"Lunch!" It was Davy again. It had taken him a few minutes to get down to number four on the list. That's record reading speed for Davy. "We have to carry our own lunch. I thought you said it wouldn't be too heavy."

Davy was a big fifth-grader. He actually would have been a pretty good-sized ninth-grader. The Regional High School football coach had taken to dropping by his house on Sundays to watch the Patriots game and talk football with Davy and his dad. Davy's lunches were something of a legend around school.

"We could just cook him when we get to the top of the mountain," said Benny, pointing to Davy. "Then none of us would have to bring a lunch, or dinner, or breakfast or lunch the next day."

"Dodgeball!" cried Davy as he grabbed a big red ball. Benny took off as fast as he could.

Chapter 3

Finally it was field trip day. The entire fifth-grade of Sanbornton Elementary School gathered along the curb in front of the school while the big yellow bus that would take us to Mount Moosilauke spewed blue exhaust into the air, idling and ready to go. Mr. Hauteman, the new science teacher, was there in tan shorts, a tan button-down shirt, and a floppy tan hat. All three were too tight, like the last time he had used them he was much younger and in much better shape. Weird bulges stuck out in every direction. His skin was kind of spongy. All right, he was an over-filled twinky. The effect was a little sickening, but to be honest, the hat was the worst. How do you gain weight in your head?

Cherilyn was there in pink shorts, pink sneakers, and a pink backpack. She was standing with Katrina, who was wearing a long canvas skirt. The two argued over whether they had to bring two makeup kits or whether they could stand to share one. They were being very obvious about how they were not looking at Melinda, who was cleaning the lens of a camera that looked more complicated than a computer. Katrina and Cherilyn always made a big show of being not interested in anything Melinda found interesting. Of course, they talked about how uninterested they were an awful lot for two people who were supposed to be uninterested.

Melinda generally ignored them, but she never mentioned it. On field trip day, she genuinely seemed not to notice Katrina and Cherilyn. She was talking to Mr. Hauteman and pointing to a series of plastic bottles and other containers laid out in front of what looked like a cross between a backpack and a toolbox.

Benny was there with a brand-new backpack that looked like the Mount Everest special from Eastern Mountain Sports: five feet tall, a dozen or more pockets and Velcro pouches, stuffed to the brim with and held together by bungee cords. He was wearing winter hiking pants and a Gore-Tex vest on this warm September morning. He had a utility belt around his waist. Hanging from the belt was a collapsible camp shovel, an aluminum camp cook set, a compass the size of a man's fist, and a coil of nylon rope. He had goggles pushed up over his knit cap. There were two or three price tags sticking out of various pieces of gear, which Mrs. Black might or might not have accidentally left attached. Benny's parents were a little sensitive about being city folks, and I bet they wanted to make sure he didn't look out of place on his first outdoor adventure. The effect would have been more convincing if Benny hadn't been wearing brown hush puppy shoes.

Davy was sitting apart, oblivious to everything going on around him, digging into a sandwich he had just pulled from an old sailor's bag, canvas and big enough to fit a body into, with a rope tie at the top and arm straps about halfway up the sides. I was sure the bag was full of food, I only wondered how long it would take for Davy to empty it and start foraging from the rest of us.

Me, I had spent three years in the Cub Scouts, so I knew a little better than most on how to be ready for a hike. Sturdy denim shorts, hiking shoes, a canvas daypack filled with a sweatshirt and windbreaker, the lunch my mom packed, a notebook and pen, a flashlight and a small first aid kit. As I finished packing that morning, I wondered if there was anything I could add to make it any more boring.

The excitement level was rising as the minutes passed and the cloud of gas belching out of the bus began to encircle the gathering crowd. Suddenly, the laughter, the chatter, the rattle of gear, all went still. Heads turned to regard a figure approaching from the teachers' parking lot; a tall, heavy-set woman in faded jeans, cotton sneakers, and a flowery cotton shirt. It could have been anyone's aunt ready for a day of gardening, but it wasn't. It was Mrs. Bartgauer. Katrina was the first to shake herself free from the shock of seeing her teacher in anything other than a large, formless, flowered cotton dress.

"Mrs. Bartgauer, I thought you weren't coming."

"I hadn't planned to," Mrs. Bartgauer replied, making an effort to sound casual and failing miserably. "But Mr. Dobson hurt his knee last night line dancing," she winced, "and Ms. Jensen is feeling under the weather, and since my whole class is going on this trip, it seems that I was the only teacher who could be spared." She looked a little bitter at the thought, and most of the fifth-grade boys looked crushed. Ms. Jensen, the young foreign language teacher, was a particular favorite with the boys, who seemed more interested in French this year than any other subject.

"If more parents had volunteered to come along, well..." Mrs. Bartgauer was now speaking more to herself than anyone else, but she seemed to shake herself back to the present and looked around. "Speaking of that, whose parents did agree to come? I heard there were two but..."

We all looked around. The few parents who

were hanging around didn't look like they were prepared to go hiking. Benny's dad was there but he wore slick-looking trousers, a silk shirt, and very expensive-looking black leather shoes. Katrina's mother was in a short skirt and high heels. It looked like she was trying to impress someone, probably someone male. But if she was trying to impress Mr. Hauteman, it was obviously not with her outdoorsy-ness. Who wasn't here yet?

Just then, a car horn blared out the Southern charge melody from "The Dukes of Hazzard" and all heads turned to see a rusted-out Chevrolet that somehow managed to raise a cloud of dust on the paved road in front of the school. It fishtailed as it spun in and screeched to a stop dangerously close to the rear bumper of the school bus.

The head and shoulders of a burly man

appeared above the roof of that dumpy old car, and he called out, "We're here. Let's get this freak show on the road!"

"Oh Harry!" called a woman with a high-pitched voice. She didn't step out of the passenger seat, she sort of uncoiled. "Be nice around the children." She said the word "children" like it had four syllables and was the name of a meal at Denny's. A bag was slung over one shoulder and she was wearing a pair of shorts and a tank top, both of which wouldn't offer much protection from the mountain brush. The huge man hefted himself out through the driver's side window without opening the door, and the ground shook when his engineer boots hit the pavement. He sauntered around and threw a hairy arm around the woman's shoulders and the two started towards the group of fifth-graders. Jimmy sprang out of the back seat and fell in beside them, matching his father's swaggering gait.

"I am NOT riding in the same bus with those people," Cherilyn said coldly, arms crossed over her chest.

Katrina turned shoulder to shoulder with her, crossed her own arms, and said, "I'm not either."

And under her breath, Mrs. Bartgauer said, "Me neither."

CHAPTER 4

The bus ride will be a story told around Sanbornton Elementary School for decades. The Whitehorses went straight to the back seat like they did it every day. No wonder – the back seat actually had both their names, encircled in a heart, carved into the plastic upholstery from when they were in school and the seat was considered theirs. When Mr. Whitehorse had been in school, whatever he claimed was his for as long as he wanted it to be.

The two had managed to walk into the bus, slip sideways down the aisle, and plop themselves down without Mr. Whitehorse ever taking his arm off his wife's shoulder. There was a rush to fill the front seats among the least adventurous of the group, Mrs. Bartgauer leading the way, but a bunch of us settled in around the weirdest chaperones in the history of Sanbornton Elementary School. With the whole fifth-grade on the trip with all their stuff, it was a bit of a tight squeeze. Everyone piled their gear in the middle, forming a wall between the back crowd and the front crowd, which seemed to satisfy all of us.

Mr. Whitehorse launched right into stories of his school-day exploits, though he never quite finished any of his stories because his wife kept cutting him off just after the story got good and just before it got really good. She would be discussing nail polish colors with some of the girls with great intensity, then suddenly spin around with a huge smile on her face and say, "Oh, Harry, you're too much."

He talked about how he and his buddies jumped the student body president, blindfolded and gagged him, and tied him to the flagpole in the middle of February. He told how they then stole the poor guy's pants. He was about to describe early stage frostbite in the most unthinkable of places when Mrs. Whitehorse jumped in. She likewise cut off a countdown of the ten best fires ever set by Sanbornton kids at number seven, the famous principal's potted plant incident of 1974. In the front of the bus, Mr. Hauteman was talking about all the great natural wonders we would see, his voice rising louder and louder every time Mr. Whitehorse's stories started to enter dangerous ground.

Jimmy was in his glory, jumping in with details of the stories he must have heard a hundred times. "That umpire was squeezing the strike zone on you all day," he prompted as his dad launched into a tale of his schoolboy pitching days.

"He sure was," his dad said, laughing loud enough to make some of the fifth-graders shrink back. "But I showed him. I told my catcher to bail out on a fastball and hit him right in the –"

"Don't even think about it, Harry!" called his wife, giggling like a schoolgirl herself.

Melinda was sitting across from me, going through a tree identification guide and drawing leaves in her notebook. I strained my neck as she flipped through a few pages and saw drawings of flowers, animal tracks, and...

"Poop!" I said, a little louder than I wanted to. All conversation stopped, and I mean immediately. Everyone in the bus turned to look, including the driver, which made the bus swerve to the left for a second before he whipped his eyes back to the road. Melinda glared up at me.

"It's called scat."

"In my world, it's called poop."

"You mean it's called –" Mr. Whitehorse said

before his wife clapped her hand over his mouth.

"When animals do it in the woods, it's called scat, and it's one way of knowing what animal species are in the environment." Melinda can sound like the "National Geographic Channel" sometimes. Mr. Hauteman, three seats away, was beaming. Melinda took one quick look at him and turned fire engine red.

"But why would you draw pictures of the stuff?" I asked.

"I'm making a notebook of all the things we might see on our hike." Melinda held up the notebook and fanned the pages.

"Wow," said Davy, "that has to be the only time you could tell someone their drawings look like crap and it would be a compliment."

That got Mrs. Bartgauer out of her seat and

storming up the aisle.

"Oops," Davy corrected himself, "I mean their drawings look like scat."

Mrs. Bartgauer reached the pile of bags and backpacks at the center of the bus and tried to step over it. Her foot caught on an arm strap and for a moment she hung in the air like a flowered cloud. Three fifth-graders dove forward to break her fall. Katrina, who was already in a position to do so, scrambled to get out of the way. Katrina may not be the bravest fifth-grader in Sanbornton, New Hampshire, but this time she might have been the smartest.

Mrs. Bartgauer hit her three rescuers, they hit the pile of gear, and the whole avalanche hit the floor in a shower of canvas, arms, and flowered cotton.

"My heavens!" cried Mrs. Bartgauer, who landed on top.

"My ankle!" cried a ponytailed girl, who landed on the bottom.

"My butt!" cried a freckle-faced boy, who landed on Benny's camp shovel.

"We're here!" cried the bus driver, looking very relieved.

CHAPTER 5

Our first casualty, and we hadn't even gotten off the bus yet. The ankle was definitely sprained, and one ponytailed girl was out of the adventure before it began.

"Lucky stiff," I heard Katrina mumble as Mr.

Hauteman finished wrapping the ankle which had already turned purplish and was starting to swell. "I wish I had thought of that."

I couldn't help but think that if Katrina had only stood her ground when Mrs. Bartgauer tried to defy gravity, she would have been at the bottom of the pile. It might have been her foot that Mr. Hauteman would have been carefully propping up on one of the bus seats.

"Hope you brought a good book," said Mr. Hauteman to the ponytailed girl. "You're grounded."

Just then, Katrina started limping around in a circle, letting out a little high-pitched moan. After a few seconds of this, she peeked up to see what kind of reaction she was getting. Everyone was looking at her, but there was more laughter and scorn in their faces than pity.

"Oh forget it," she snarled and grabbed her backpack.

Everyone else did the same, and there were "oofs" and "ughs" as one by one the fifth-graders of Sanbornton Elementary School shouldered their bags and crowded up. There was a louder, angrier sound as Benny swung his bag over his shoulder, staggered under the shifting weight, and slammed into a much bigger boy. The larger boy had already reared back for a roundhouse punch when he was suddenly lifted clean off his feet by one enormous hand attached to the tattooed arm of Mr. Whitehorse. As the boy hung, arms and legs flapping in the air, Mrs. Whitehorse stepped up in front of him, fists planted on her hips.

"Now, now, young man. Violence doesn't solve anything."

"Yeah, any moron knows that," said her son Jimmy, walking past and backhanding the hanging boy in the gut. The wind came out of him in an audible whoosh, and Mr. Whitehorse dropped him in a heap on the ground. Then Mr. Whitehorse threw one arm around his wife, planted the other across his son's shoulders, and the three sauntered off together, the picture of the perfect family.

CHAPTER 6

Mr. Hauteman handed out clear plastic zip-top baggies.

"Now you each are to take three samples. Make sure everything you take is off the ground — no picking live plants — and no living animals."

"And no scat," sneered Davy, just behind Melinda's ear. She jabbed him in the ribs with a quick elbow. "Hey!" he cried, pointing to Melinda and looking out of habit to the parent chaperones.

Mrs. Whitehorse rapped him off the back of the head and said, "You probably deserved it."

"Now stay together," called Mr. Hauteman, trying to keep the attention of the group on him. "We will travel at the speed of the slowest member of the group. Mrs. Bartgauer and I will lead the way, and Mr. and Mrs. Whitehorse will go last. You must stay between us. I'll call for rests every so often, but if you need a break, just call 'break' and we'll all stop. OK? Let's go!" And with a wave of his hand, he turned and set his boot on the path.

"Break!" called Benny, slumping to the ground. He whipped off his knit cap, letting loose a flood of sweat that beaded up on the artificial fabric of his vest. Half the fifth-graders started to laugh; the other half plopped themselves down on the ground. Mr. Hauteman strode back to stand in front of the puffing Benny.

"What do you mean 'break'? You haven't taken a single step!"

Then he noticed how white Benny's face was, and Mr. Hauteman went from anger to fear in a flash.

"You're dehydrating. Quick, out of that winter gear."

If possible, Benny's face went even whiter. He started to croak something, but Mr. Hauteman had already pushed his pack off his back, stripped off the vest, and was pulling at the winter weather outer pants. They caught, of course, on the hush puppies, and Mr. Hauteman was too busy trying to free them and calling for water to notice what every fifth-grader immediately saw. Benny flipped over and started to scramble to his feet, hands covering far too little of the teddy bear boxers, which were all he was wearing underneath.

Mr. Hauteman was still holding the nylon pants when Benny tried to rise to his feet. Immediately, his legs went out from under him and he went down as rigid as a tree, planting his face on the rocky ground. Blood spurted from his nose, and the laughter that had erupted at the sight of his printed underwear seemed to be sucked back in by thirty mouths. There was a beat as the world before Benny's fall ended and a whole new one began. Then Davy puked.

Too many tuna fish sandwiches, too much excitement, and the shock of going from laughter to the sharp intake of breath was too hard on his system – it just had to happen, I guess. Of course, it probably didn't have to happen on Cherilyn's pink sneakers, but sometimes the world just makes sense. Cherilyn screamed. Marjorie Jackson, all five foot six of her, went white and wavered. It might have been a strong breeze buffeting her the way her head and shoulders moved while her feet stayed planted. I leapt to catch her. Another boy leapt too. Marjorie passed the tipping point and fainted away, arms swinging in a perfect display of centrifugal motion as she pinwheeled toward the ground. I caught Marjorie's head in my hands. The other boy caught her right hand with his face.

"My goodness," squeaked Mrs. Whitehorse, "they're dropping like flies. At this rate, there won't be anyone left to climb the mountain."

Katrina seemed to consider this statement for a second, then her arms flew up in the air and she spun a few times on her toes, a little like my five-year-old sister did in her first ballet recital. She let out a little, high-pitched cry, and slumped dramatically to the ground. It would have been more convincing if she hadn't placed her hands so carefully on the grass just before her shoulders touched down lightly. Nobody leapt to catch her.

Katrina lay on the ground for a few seconds while we all stared down at her, the other spectacles temporarily forgotten in favor of this virtuoso performance. After a full three seconds, she peeked out through slitted eyelids to see what effect her faint had made on her audience. Jimmy started to clap hesitantly.

"Oh forget it," she snarled and stood up, brushing off her clothes.

CHAPTER 7

It took Mr. Hauteman fifteen minutes to sort out the latest casualties. Benny wasn't going anywhere. He bubbled at the mouth as the bus driver poured water into him. He then described a kitty cat he kept hidden from the building supervisor, clearly back in his old Manhattan apartment. Marjorie insisted she was all right for a little while then agreed to stay behind and minister to the boy she had clocked and his broken nose. Marjorie always seemed to be injuring someone around her; she wasn't the most coordinated person in Sanbornton.

One time in industrial arts she managed to pound three fingers with a hammer in a single class period. Only one of them was hers. Come to think of it, the boy she hit probably got off easy. His eye had swollen so badly he couldn't see out of it, and, as Mr. Hauteman pointed out, one-eyed hikers near cliffs was one thing he did not need.

While Marjorie tried to argue herself back onto the hike, Davy lobbied pretty hard to be off it. He did look terribly green, and Mr. Hauteman started to point him back to the bus, but Mr. Whitehorse stepped in and clamped a meaty hand on Davy's even meatier shoulder.

"Ah, a big guy like this can hack it," Mr. Whitehorse boomed. "What he really needs is some fresh mountain air, right?" It seems those big guys have a thing, some brotherhood of the bruisers. Davy started to object, but Mr. Whitehorse gave him a huge grin and a squeeze on the shoulder that lifted him clean off the ground. He swallowed hard and nodded.

"If he's going up, so am I," chipped in Jimmy. "I wouldn't want to be below him if he sees any more blood. I didn't bring an umbrella."

Four students were now splayed out on seats of the big yellow school bus, and we had yet to get on the trail. I started to think that the expedition was cursed. Mrs. Bartgauer mumbled something about her being cursed. Davy just cursed. Mr. Hauteman seemed to be in a hurry to get us going. I wondered if he actually thought we would be safer up on the side of a mountain.

CHAPTER 8

As it turns out, danger was wherever the fifth-grade of Sanbornton Elementary School was. We weren't half a mile up the trail before Mrs. Bartgauer had to break up a knot of kids. They were clustered around a boy who was kneeling on the ground, drawing pictures in the dirt and telling horror stories of the deep woods.

"The North American Ambush Viper," he lectured, trying to make his voice sound deep, though it was in the process of cracking. The result sounded like a cross between Dracula and a hyena.

"It is five feet long, shiny black with a silvery head. It hides in trees and drops on its victims without warning. The venom from a single bite can cause a grown man's skin to turn purple and his hair to fall out, and he will die a violent, painful death. There is no known antidoooooh!"

The boy wailed as Mrs. Bartgauer grabbed one ear and hauled him to his feet.

"If your feet moved as fast as your mouth, you'd be at the top of the mountain by now. And where do you get off telling such wild lies?"

"It's not a lie! I read all about the North American Ambush Viper in one of those books Melinda's been carrying around all week."

At the invocation of the authority of a book, all the other fifth-graders went wide-eyed, their mouths hanging open in shock and fear. They might not all have been big readers, but they knew one thing for sure. If it was in a book, it must be true. And having someone else read the book and report the findings was something they understood. Isn't that what Mrs. Bartgauer made them do every week in English class?

"Go ahead. Ask Melinda. She knows everything ever written about the woods." He looked up at Melinda hopefully, and I swear he winked. First Cherilyn and then him, it must be catchy.

Melinda gave him a disgusted sneer, shook her head, and walked on by. It sounded ridiculous to me, but I noticed she didn't actually deny the existence of the North American Ambush Viper, and that made me nervous. Apparently, Mrs. Bartgauer noticed this too, and her eyes wandered to the branches overhanging the trail. Her hand rose involuntarily, as if to ward off a sudden attack, but she forgot she was still holding a fifth-grader's ear.

"Oooowwww!" he cried, and Mrs. Bartgauer let him fall to the ground. She walked on, never letting her eyes drift from the canopy of trees.

The horsing around went on like that for the first half-hour of the hike, but the whole expedition got quiet fast when the trail sloped up sharply. All of a sudden, I found myself drenched in sweat. We had done some hiking in Cub Scouts, but that was walking in the woods. This was climbing. I was amazed at how quickly I was getting tired until I noticed that I had gone from nearly the back of the line to within a few people of the front, passing fifth-graders in various stages of incapacitation along the way.

Fifth-graders were melting before my eyes. They were taking off sweaters and sweatshirts, pouring water bottles over their heads, plopping down on rocks that were suddenly too high to climb over. And in the lead, Mr. Hauteman, stepping lightly and sprightly, thumbs hooked in the straps of his pack, head bobbing to a tune only he could hear. Melinda fell into step behind him and beside me, head bobbing along with Mr. Hauteman's.

The miles just seemed to be crawling by, and the line of fifth-graders stretched out farther and farther. The path just got steeper and steeper, and still, all we could see were trees and rocks, rocks and trees. My knees ached. Every muscle in my legs was cramping. The constant pain was combining with the endless monotony of the scenery to make my mind go numb. Still, for every rock I climbed over, there seemed to be a hundred more sprouting out from the very ground. I took it for as long as I could; then I took it for a lifetime more. Finally, I felt like I was at the end of my rope.

I turned to Melinda and asked, "How many hours have we been on this trail?"

"One," she answered, not even bothering to turn and look at me.

That woke me up and gave me something to think about. I was still trying to figure out when and how time stopped, when a scream came from several hundred feet back. Mr. Hauteman seemed to be yanked back as if he were on a leash. He spun around and charged past us back down the trail. Some of the fifth-graders started drifting back after him, but most just watched him go by and collapsed where they stood.

Later, I heard what Mr. Hauteman found when he got back to the center of the storm. An unsuspecting fifth-grade boy was trudging up the hill when a long, black shape fell on him from a branch above his head. Something cold and hard bit into his cheek, and he screamed. He went down, grabbing at the sinewy figure that was wrapped around his neck.

"Snake! Snake! Ambush Viper!"

Panic radiated from the spot. Mrs. Bartgauer, eyes glued to the overhanging branches, had fallen farther and farther back. She tripped on the squirming boy and sprawled over him. Fifth-graders ran in every direction. The boy who had been giving the lesson on the fictional North American Ambush Viper dropped down from the tree where the attack had come from, no belt now on his jeans, laughing and pointing at the helpless victim struggling for breath beneath the prone figure of Mrs. Bartgauer.

He was so amused with his little joke that he didn't notice Jimmy sneaking up on one side and Davy on the other. One quick tug from each on his beltless jeans and the pants were down around his ankles. He yelled in anger and lunged at them, but tripped and fell. Davy and Jimmy ran on up the trail, whooping with triumph. Melinda and I moved to the edges of the path to let them run on past us. Cherilyn and Katrina turned their backs on the commotion and trudged up the trail behind them.

"I can't believe how immature some of my classmates can be," Cherilyn muttered.

"Me neither," Katrina chimed in.

Melinda just shrugged and we followed behind them.

CHAPTER 9

"It looks a little like jello," said Davy, still on his favorite subject, food.

He and Jimmy huddled over a pile of something just off the edge of the trail. Katrina and Cherilyn were both leaning forward and hanging back, perfectly balanced between curiosity and revulsion. Melinda and I stood in the middle of the trail, looking back downhill for the rest of the class. They were nowhere to be seen.

Jimmy snorted. "Don't be a moron. Jello isn't brown and no one would bring jello up a mountain."

"Why not? I brought pudding snacks, and they're brown," crowed Davy, pulling a plastic package from his pocket and waving it proudly as if that won him the argument once and for all.

"Well, if you think it looks like jello, why don't you taste it?" Jimmy challenged, clearly not blown over by the force of the big boy's logic.

There was a second's hesitation, and then Davy seemed to weigh the greatly depleted feedbag on his back. One hand ran over it, feeling the beloved shapes of sandwiches, snack packs, and sodas. I could see his lips move as he listed out his remaining food items in his head. Disappointment filled his face as he came to the end of the list. He leaned a little forward and gave the pile a sniff.

"Oh, gross!" yelled Katrina.

"Hey, there's a zipper in there," said Davy, pointing at the pile, "and a bottle cap and something that looks like part of a tuna can."

"A zipper?" cried Mrs. Bartgauer, who had just caught up with us and was leaning over with her hands on her knees, trying to catch her breath.

"Don't touch that!" Melinda screamed. "It's bear scat!"

Davy looked up dully, not seeming to register

her words. "What was that?" he asked.

Jimmy got it. He stuttered a second, then pointed straight at the jiggling pile and cried, "Bear poop!"

Davy leapt back, arms flailing, head whipping around wildly. He tripped and would have fallen if he hadn't run up against something large and soft.

Jimmy raised his pointing finger from the pile on the ground to a spot just inches above Davy's head. "Bear!" he cried.

CHAPTER 10

Davy froze, then slowly swiveled his head. The creature responsible for the brown jello pile was standing on his hind legs, his front paws resting on the trunk of a good-sized pine tree. Davy's muscles seemed to contract all at once. He looked like he was trying to shrink into a smaller space, as if the bear wouldn't notice the largest piece of meat it had ever run into. The pudding snack cup exploded in Davy's clenching hand.

Pudding sprayed everywhere – on the ground, the trees, the bear, and, probably most disturbing, on Davy. Time seemed to stop as the bear sniffed the air and Davy began to work out the implications of this latest development. Then the bear's head moved forward, and everybody scattered.

I headed for the nearest tree – a good, tall birch – but I heard Melinda's voice behind me, stronger and more forceful than I could ever have imagined.

"No, Escapade, not up there."

I looked back and she was pointing above my head. I looked up and saw deep gashes in the bark of the tree about six feet above the ground.

"Claw marks," Melinda called. "The bear marked that tree. We're in his territory."

Melinda ran past me up the trail and I got the hint. I gave up the idea of climbing and ran after her.

I was running forward but looking backwards, expecting the bear to loom over me at any second. I tripped twice, scraped both knees and the palms of my hands raw, but kept scrambling up and running. Melinda got farther ahead of me every time I went down until I could only catch glimpses of her when the trail straightened out. A side path branched to the left, and I only saw the pack she was wearing as she turned. I followed her off the main trail, but the side path seemed to leap straight up, and I scrambled on hands and feet to get over the rocks.

"Come on!" Melinda called. "The steeper, the better. Bears will take the easiest path."

"Smart animals," I mumbled between pants as my lungs punished me for every ragged breath. The first time the path flattened out, I threw myself down, sucking in air the way Davy sucks in cake. After six or seven gargantuan breaths, I leapt back on my feet, looking for the next step up.

There wasn't one. The path ended on the rounded top of the rock on which I stood. Melinda stood four feet in front of me, frozen against the endless blue sky that was all that was left at the edge of the mountain.

CHAPTER 11

Melinda took my picture on the rock looking over the edge of Mount Moosilauke. Then I took her picture. We didn't say a word for a long time. The sound of the wind whipping free over the summit somehow made it sound quieter, and the view was amazing. Four thousand feet below, it seemed like the whole world was covered in trees. It was a little lonely, but somehow that was OK.

We were staring out at the other peaks, standing up like chessmen from the lowlands below, when we heard a wheezing kind of pant behind us. I'll admit it, I panicked.

"Bear!" I cried.

"Where?" weezed Mrs. Bartgauer, who was actually crawling up the last few feet of the trail, using her hands to pull herself onto the rounded summit of the mountain. There were tears in her eyes as she looked up at us. Melinda clearly looked shocked.

"Is it you, Mrs. Bartgauer?"

"Am I dead?" she asked, and laid her cheek down on the stone pillow of Mount Moosilauke.

"Where's the bear?" I asked as I knelt down beside the heaving flowered shirt.

"Haven't seen it," she gasped. "It was licking Davy last time I saw it."

Melinda and I looked quickly at each other. Delusional. That was the word we had heard in health class. Mrs. Bartgauer was so dehydrated and stressed that she was seeing things.

"Are you sure the bear wasn't chasing you?" Melinda asked softly, carefully.

"I was chasing you two!" Mrs. Bartgauer shouted, suddenly energized by her teacherly duties. "You aren't supposed to go on without a teacher. Think of what could have happened to you."

"We could have NOT been eaten by a bear," I pointed out. Mrs. Bartgauer pondered that for a second, nodded, and put her head back down on the rock.

When Mrs. Bartgauer caught her breath, we knew it was time to go down. We couldn't wait on the mountain all day, and we certainly didn't want to be there at night. I looked at Melinda, and she looked at me, and we just started walking back down the trail. Mrs. Bartgauer gave a little whine, but she pulled herself to her feet and followed us down. She came slowly and was quickly out of sight behind us, but she came.

I was amazed at how steep the trail was. I wasn't thinking about it in the mad rush up, but now I felt every jolt as I dropped from rock to rock. The tension of looking for a wall of fur wasn't helping. Suddenly I stopped dead and I pointed to a tall birch tree with jagged scars on its trunk about six feet above the ground.

"This is where the bear was," I whispered.

"Oh, don't worry," Melinda said in her normal, cheerful voice. "That was a black bear, and black bears don't usually hang around people. I'll bet he's five miles from here by now."

"How do you know?"

"I read it in one of those nature books Mr. Hauteman suggested, the ones you guys thought were so boring."

"Well, if you knew bears were so safe, why did you run?"

"Because there was a bear, dummy! What did you expect me to do?"

I looked at her and shook my head. I just don't understand girls, and I hope I never will. I don't want things like that to make sense.

"Where do you suppose the rest of the guys are?" I asked. "Do you think they went up the mountain?"

"I doubt it. We'd have seen them as we came down."

"You guys may think the bear is gone," came a high, nervous voice from above, "but we're not coming down until we're sure."

We looked up and saw Davy, Jimmy, Katrina, and Cherilyn clinging to tree trunks at least ten feet above the ground. And, amazingly, so was Mr. Hauteman and most of the fifth-grade of Sanbornton Elementary School.

"What are you guys doing up there?" Melinda asked as some of the fifth-graders started to climb down.

"We heard yelling ahead, so we rushed up,"

said Mr. Hauteman in a shaky voice. "And there was this enormous b-b-b-ear!"

"It tried to eat Davy," called out one of the boys.

"I was covered in pudding! It licked me like a lollipop," moaned Davy, who hadn't managed to scramble more than four feet up a pine tree.

"It was gonna eat him," chirped in one of the girls. "Then it went after his lunch instead."

All eyes turned to the shredded remains of Davy's sailor's bag. Melinda walked over and stared down at the carnage.

"Do you like peanut butter sandwiches, Davy?" she asked.

"Yeah," he said warily.

"Do they taste good?"

"Yeah, sure."

"Well, now you have another reason to like them, and you should be thankful that the bear likes them too. Apparently peanut butter sandwiches smell – and taste – better than you do."

It was a line that Benny himself would have been proud of.

CHAPTER 12

It took a few minutes for Melinda to explain that black bears don't really eat people, which eventually convinced two-thirds of the class to come out of their trees. It took another minute to explain that black bears are excellent tree climbers, and that brought the rest of them down in a hurry.

Mr. Hauteman was the only one left in a tree, and he was clutching onto the trunk so hard he was probably leaving claw marks of his own.

"He's cracked," mumbled a boy as he stared up at his science teacher. "He'll never make it up the mountain now."

Katrina seemed to perk up at that and she rushed to the trunk of a nearby beech tree. Wrapping her arms and legs around the trunk, she threw her head back and wailed, "I can't take it! I can't take it, I tell you. I'm scared! There must be a hundred bears up that trail just waiting to eat us all!"

Her cries faded out as she pressed her cheek against the rough bark and snuck a peek out of the corner of one eye at her classmates. No one looked overly concerned.

"Katrina, how could you?" sneered one girl, nodding quickly at Mr. Hauteman, who had shrunken at the plaintive sound of Katrina's voice.

"Oh forget it," Katrina snarled. She let go of the trunk, crossed her arms, and leaned against the tree instead.

Mrs. Bartgauer appeared just then, stumbling down the trail and collapsing onto a rock. She raised a hand as if calling for attention, but her ragged breaths would not let her speak.

"I think we are turning back anyway, Katrina," said an exasperated Melinda. "We are going back down now, aren't we?" Melinda turned and spoke to Mr. Hauteman like she was calming a frightened kitten.

Mrs. Bartgauer looked up, eyes wide. "Now?" she whimpered.

Mr. Hauteman looked so thankful as he gazed into Melinda's eyes, like he was that frightened kitten and wanted to bury himself in Melinda's arms. I'm not used to seeing parents, teachers even, looking so helpless. I felt kind of weird, like this was something I should be looking away from. Mr. Hauteman nodded and Melinda held out her hand. Mr. Hauteman took it with just his fingertips and meekly started following Melinda down the trail. We all fell in silently behind them.

We hadn't gone more than a quarter of a mile when we heard a deep, booming noise coming from just around the next bend.

"The bear!" cried Cherilyn, and she dashed into the trees beside the trail.

Mr. Hauteman gave a shriek and crouched low behind one of Melinda's legs.

The rest of us stopped and stared, frozen in place, while the growling racket slowly jelled into a human voice, and then into song.

"My uncle, he was a lonely man
Ten years he lived in the lonely land
All he owned was his trusty mule
All the county called him a fool
He made his camp 'neath those mountain
    scenes
He drank his coffee and ate his beans
Back to the fire he passed some gas
The fire bloomed and burnt his—"

"Oh, Harry!" cried Mrs. Whitehorse, reaching down to cover her husband's mouth from her perch on his shoulders as the two came around the corner just as casually as you please. Mr. Whitehorse laughed as he shook her palms from his mouth and looked up with a grin and then noticed the whole fifth-grade class standing silently on the trail in front of him.

"What?" he cried. "Are we done already?"

"Argh!" cried Mrs. Bartgauer and she pushed her way through the group, gave Mr. Whitehorse a healthy shove, and, for the first time all day, took the lead. Mr. Whitehorse backpedaled. Mrs. Whitehorse waved her hands, struggling for balance. Her husband lurched to catch her. He did, but she pulled him off balance. Katrina, standing right behind the couple, screamed and shielded her face with her hands. All three went down in a heap.

CHAPTER 13

We got back a half an hour before the final bell. The principal, Mrs. Lissard, had called the whole school together for an assembly so we could tell them about the field trip. They were already sitting in the bleachers when we all straggled towards the row of chairs facing the crowd. What a sight we must have been!

Most of us were scratched and ruffled. There was Benny in his winter weather outfit, open and unzipped to the edge of social acceptability. Marjorie was still holding a bloody towel to her victim's nose. Katrina was being carried by Mr. Whitehorse yet was still trying to get as far away from him as possible. One ponytailed girl hopped on one foot, using a branch for a crutch. Jimmy rode on his mother's shoulders, a straw in his mouth for effect. Davy looked, well, like he had been licked by a bear.

"What happened to you?" Mrs. Lissard asked as we, the entire fifth-grade, slumped into the folding chairs and dropped our gear all around us. She fixed her gaze on Mr. Hauteman, who had slowly stopped shaking during the bus ride back but was clearly not back to his usual self. He answered in a halting, cracked voice.

"Bear. Big bear. Bad bear. Big bad bear." And that was all he could say before he collapsed into a chair of his own.

Mrs. Lissard looked shocked. "Is everyone OK?" she asked, to no one and to everyone. Mrs. Whitehorse was the one who answered, in her piercing, window-rattling voice.

"Oh honey, we all just came through fine. Don't you worry. I don't think any of the bones are actually broken."

Mrs. Lissard blanched, but she made a quick survey with her eyes and saw that everyone seemed to be there and in one piece.

"Did anyone actually make it up the mountain?"

Everyone turned to look at Melinda and me, then hands reached out and pushed us forward.

Melinda pulled out her digital camera and started showing pictures in her viewfinder to kids in the front. There was a scramble of bodies and a chorus of "oohs" and "aahs" over the views from the top of Mount Moosilauke. She also had a lot to say about how the big bad bear turned out to be very gentle when he licked Davy clean of pudding and was, like Davy himself, just a little hungry.

When she was done, Mrs. Lissard put her hands on Melinda's and my shoulders and introduced us as being the only members of Sanbornton Elementary School to successfully climb Mount Moosilauke. The entire assembly rose to its feet. They cheered, they clapped, they hooted. Standing in front of my whole school, feeling my face get hot, I didn't know if it was the best day of my life or the worst. Suddenly I remembered that something was wrong.

"But Mrs. Lissard," I said, my voice rising to a shout to be heard over the cheering crowd, "someone else made it to the top."

Mrs. Lissard quieted the crowd with a wave of her hands. "Who? I didn't see anyone else in the pictures."

"Mrs. Bartgauer," Melinda said. "She was there, too."

Frankly, Mrs. Lissard looked a little stunned. OK, the whole assembly looked stunned, but the principal recovered quickly and called out, "Let's have Mrs. Bartgauer up here, too, then."

There were a few seconds of nervous coughing and shuffling of feet as all the kids looked around for Mrs. Bartgauer. It took everyone a heartbeat to realize they were looking at her. It wasn't the jeans or the cotton sneakers that made her so unrecognizable as the woman who had held sway over the fifth-grade for more than two decades in Sanbornton. It wasn't even the caked mud, the leaves in her hair, or the scratches up and down her arms. It was the look in her eyes; it was the way she clenched her hands as she strode forward.

She looked ragged, harried, and mad. No more was she the frightened, nervous old woman begging for quiet. She would have quiet, if that was what she wanted. She was a force of nature.

And she looked great. I felt a little stirring of pride that this was MY teacher. Mrs. Bartgauer marched up to the principal and stood tall and straight beside her.

"Did you really make it all the way to the top of Mount Moosilauke, despite the bear, injuries, and heaven knows what else went on up there, when most of the field trip didn't?" the principal asked.

"I did," was the short reply.

"And what will you remember from this trip?"

"I will remember, every time one of you fifth-graders gives me any lip," she turned to look up and down the row of metal chairs, "that I faced down a bear and still made it to the top of the mountain while most of you didn't. You'd better remember that, too."

And without another word, Mrs. Bartgauer stalked out of the gym. Life was not ever going to be the same for the fifth-grade of Sanbornton Elementary School.

EPILOGUE

It's nine o'clock at night now, and school is more than six hours in the past. Mom's American chop suey tasted better than it ever did before. I guess I was pretty hungry. I'm sitting at the desk in my room with my feet soaking in a bucket of hot water. I think one of my toenails is going to fall off. If it goes, I won't be able to wait until school tomorrow to show it off.

This is a great time to sit at my computer and write down everything that happened today. I figure I can hand in bits of it to Mrs. Bartgauer for my English essay, and some other bits to Mr. Hauteman for my science paper. Some of it, though, I'll save and put into my first book. After today, I'm sure about one thing; I'd much rather be a writer than a mountain climber.

Still, I stood on top of a mountain today. I looked down on all the places where normal life happens. I was above it all, even if it was for just a few minutes. And I stood in front of my whole school while everyone clapped and cheered. That is a good thing, I think. And maybe, just once in my life, it is worth living up to my name.

That's all for today from Escapade Johnson – famous writer, fearless mountain climber, bear tamer. Look for more from me as soon as anything happens at Sanbornton Elementary School, the most boring school in the most boring town in the most boring state in the whole wide world.

About the Author

Michael Sullivan is a storyteller, juggler, chess instructor, librarian, and former school teacher who grew up in small town New Hampshire, and now lives in Portsmouth, NH. He has worked with kids in many settings, from summer camps to the Boston Museum of Science, and is rumored to have once been a kid himself. He is the author of the book *Connecting Boys With Books*, and speaks across the country on the topic of boys and reading. In 1998, he was chosen New Hampshire Librarian of the Year.

Visit Michael's website at:
http://www.talestoldtall.com/BoyMeetsBook.html

Coming soon...*Escapade Johnson and The Coffee Shop of the Living Dead*

As a rule, I don't get into a whole lot of trouble. It's not that I'm a real goodie-goodie, it's just that I don't always jump at the opportunity when it comes along. I'll see a chance to do something really cool, and while I'm thinking about doing it, the chance just sort of goes away. Not in my next book, though. I join The Great Fifth Grade Homework Strike, have a major run-in with a sprinkler system and two girls, cause the biggest traffic accident in Sanbornton history, and am sentenced to ten weeks in The Coffee Shop of the Living Dead! I don't know how I'm going to survive this.